Corpses

VIK SHIRLEY

A SUBLUNARY OBJECT

ISBN 978-0-578-64221-5

Third printing.

Manufactured in the United States of America
Printed on acid-free paper
First published by Sublunary Editions in 2020
Design and typesetting by Joshua Rothes

Sublunary Editions
Seattle, WA
sublunaryeditions.com

Acknowledgements

Thanks to Joshua Rothes, Luke Palmer, Luke Kennard and Owen Shirley for their comments on this manuscript.

CORPSES

Each one of us is a synthesis of the real and unreal. We all wear a guise. Even within our own minds, we make constant efforts to conceal ourselves from ourselves, only to be repeatedly found out.

Charles Simic

I have achieved a tremendous fall.
I've lost the ability to work.
Completely. I'm a living corpse.
Abba, Father, I have fallen. Help me. To Rise.

Daniil Kharms

1.

Corpses dangled from hanging-basket hooks around the village. The lost and found at the station contained ears, tongues and body parts. The reality show was getting all of this, it was really great stuff, but the production team were feeling increasingly anxious.

2.

The way the corpses were stacked meant the faces were positioned towards the would-be couple's place of business, which made it hard for them to indulge in the racy banter that had kept them going these previous months.

3.

She dressed two of the corpses in Grandmother's petticoats and smeared lipstick over their faces and teeth. She moulded Play-Doh to her favourite corpse's thumb to replicate Grandmother's, which was permanently swollen, having been caught in a mangle some time in the 1950s.

4.

The corpses rolled around in the back of the van and got *quite* the rhythm on-the-go back there. "Infectious as hell!", said little Pete, but it didn't take much to get him going.

5.

The temperature up on the mountain kept the decomposition at a more manageable rate, so that Walter was able to relax his schedule. Their daily chats turned to weekly chats, or just as often as he could get up there, now that the housework was solely his responsibility.

6.

She rolled the corpse up tightly in the rug, just like she'd seen a million times in the movies. Her arthritis allowed her to drag it as far as the edge of the garden pond, and she sat out there most summer evenings, until the body putrified and collapsed beneath her weight.

7.

"Corpses were corpses were corpses", the old man sang, but the fact that he was still singing after death put his theory into question.

8.

Roger's corpse was as disruptive and cumbersome as he had been in person, Patrice thought, as the coroner *finally* transferred his body to the morgue.

9.

The mass grave was overcrowded and didn't give any individual corpse the opportunity to shine, unless a loved one had chosen to lacquer them heavily before saying their goodbyes. But lacquer had been hard to come by for weeks now, along with sausage skin, mildew spray and anchovies.

10.

The corpses fell from the ceiling of the cave entrance, like a beaded curtain. They were wrapped in what can only be described as Christmas tree netting.

11.

The stepping stones were frozen corpses; there was no other way across the lake. Their hearts quickened as they could hear the dogs, now not so far away, in the distance.

The child coated the corpse with a thin layer of yogurt, added some marmalade sprinkled with fish food, and inserted several birthday cake candles into the cold and hardening flesh. He hoped his mother would help him ignite them, so that he could blow them all out at the party.

13.

She knew she had made a fool of herself. Said too much, *shown* too much. Made too much of the once limp, now finally stiff, morsel that had enticed her here in the first place. Well, at least she knew her secret was safe, she thought, unaware of the CCTV cameras in every room of the funeral parlour.

The fitness-class programme stated that dancing with corpses was actually very good for your core strength and balance.

15.

"A forest of corpses", "a lake of cadavers", "a sky of stiffs", the poet didn't really know where she was going with this.

16.

She named him Frasier and found his psychiatric services more financially manageable than her last therapist, while his listening skills were second to none

17.

The birds made a home in the corpses in the trees, the field mice in the corpses in the bushes, the fish within the corpses in the lake and so on.

The survivors used the corpses of their friends as blankets and the bandleader tried to get some kind of sing-along started. But only one of the seven of them joined in, so they didn't get much momentum going and morale, if anything, plummeted.

19.

The mortician made an excuse and left the room when the family came to view the corpse. For the deceased's friends had thought he was sleeping and had written DICKHEAD on his forehead in permanent marker.

Don't know what it was about this one, but the Grim Reaper couldn't move on. He had to be prised from the corpse by his assistant, who was female and much better at the job. She was embarrassed for him, really, and had seen it coming. "Just fucking step down, for fucks sake", she muttered, as he coughed and wept and spluttered, slowly allowing himself to be peeled off the pool attendant's body.

21.

Marjorie asked for a corpse for Christmas. As usual, Todd made *that* face at her. He did it last year, when she'd asked for Mr Frosty.

22.

In the dream, the corpses were like pastel-coloured Stickle Bricks, which slotted and meshed together, and had no distinct fragrance.

23.

She propped him up, straightened his hat, and off they went through the tunnel of love.

The private investigator was disappointed. Would he still get his money for nothing more than a roomful of corpses?

25.

Corpse world! Visit today, lay with the greats, or at least their papier-mâché doppelgängers. A bit like Pompeii, but the people were never there in the first place.

26.

'Rhapsody in Blue' always took Eva back to her tending-to-corpses years.

27.

At the hog roast, Terrance kept getting flashbacks to the suite of corpses he'd encountered, by chance, as a child. His partner watched his face flinch and contort and wished he wasn't *quite* so opposed to the idea of therapy.

She had charcoal drawings of the corpses scattered around her room, miniature models of corpses, half of which she had already hand-painted, on her table, and an assortment of blow-up corpses within easy reach of her bed.

29.

Oysters and champagne, corpses by candlelight. Esther and Graham had thought Teresa had said '*corsets* by candlelight' so were a little shocked at the open caskets when they arrived in their lingerie for what they understood was a swingers' party.

It was an initiation. First you had to spend a night with a corpse, then a week, then a month and then a year. It would have been alright if they'd at least switched up the corpses, but for those with commitment issues, this set-up was particularly cruel.

Vik Shirley is a poet from Bristol currently studying for a PhD in 'Dark Humour and the Surreal in Poetry' at the University of Birmingham. Her first collection, *The Continued Closure of the Blue Door*, will be published by HVTN Press in 2020, as will her Hesterglock Press pamphlet, *Disrupted Blue and Other Poems on Polaroid*. Her work has appeared in such places as *Queen Mob's Teahouse*, *Shearsman*, *3:AM Magazine*, *Tears in the Fence*, *The Interpreters House*, *Dostoyevsky Wannabe Cities: Bristol*, and the Verve Poetry Press anthology, *It All Radiates Outwards*. She is Assistant Prose Poetry Editor of *Pithead Chapel*.

The Posthumous Works of Thomas Pilaster
Éric Chevillard, tr. Chris Clarke

A Cage for Every Child
S. D. Chrostowska

Morsel May Sleep
Ellen Dillon

Homecoming
Magda Isanos, tr. Christina Tudor-Sideri

A Book of Madness
Fernando Pessoa

Rationalism
Douglus Luman

Anecdotes
Heinrich von Kleist, tr. Matthew Spencer